Christmas 1983

To Adrienne

from

Grandma Lil

For Mom & Dad
(who taught me how to hug)

A Book of Hugs

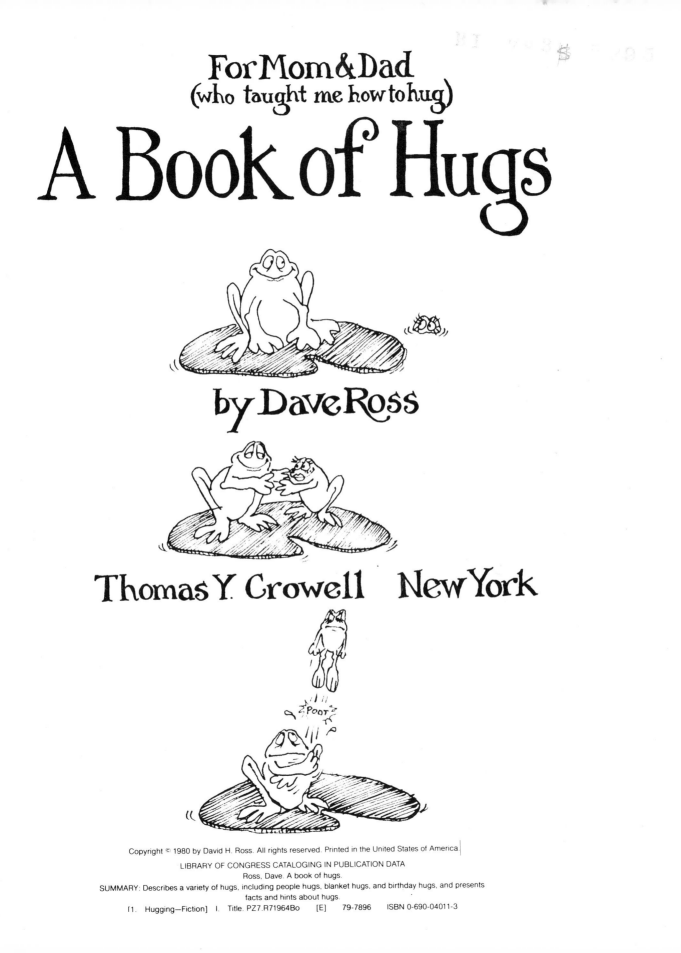

by Dave Ross

Thomas Y. Crowell   New York

LIBRARY OF CONGRESS CATALOGING IN PUBLICATION DATA
Ross, Dave. A book of hugs.
SUMMARY: Describes a variety of hugs, including people hugs, blanket hugs, and birthday hugs, and presents
facts and hints about hugs.
[1. Hugging—Fiction] I. Title. PZ7.R71964Bo [E] 79-7896 ISBN 0-690-04011-3

hug (həg), *v.*, hugged, hug·ging —*v.t.* **1.** To clasp a person or thing in one's arms; to embrace [? Scand; cf. Icel *hugga* to soothe, console; akin to OE *hogian* to care for] — *n.* an embrace

hugger, *n.*, one who hugs [*see* A]—Ant., huggee [Obs.] a person or thing that receives a hug [*see* B]

huggable, adj., possessing an affectionate nature or qualities desirable to hug [*see* fig. 1]—Ant., unhuggable [*see* fig. 2]

figure 1

figure 2

Animal Hugs
Fish Hugs

Fish hugs are very cold and seldom returned.
P.S. Never hug a shark,.

Three kinds of Bear Hugs

(bare!)

Bear hugs are very strong. Be careful not to hurt.

Octopus Hug

An octopus hugs with its whole body.

Porcupine Hug

Porcupine hugs are done very carefully.

Puppy Hugs

Puppy hugs are very soft and wet.

Fraidycat Hugs

Fraidycat hugs make you feel safe.

Piggyback Hug*

* Sometimes called riding piggyback.

A good way to travel or see a parade.

People Hugs
Mommy Hugs

You can never hug a Mommy too much.

Daddy Hug

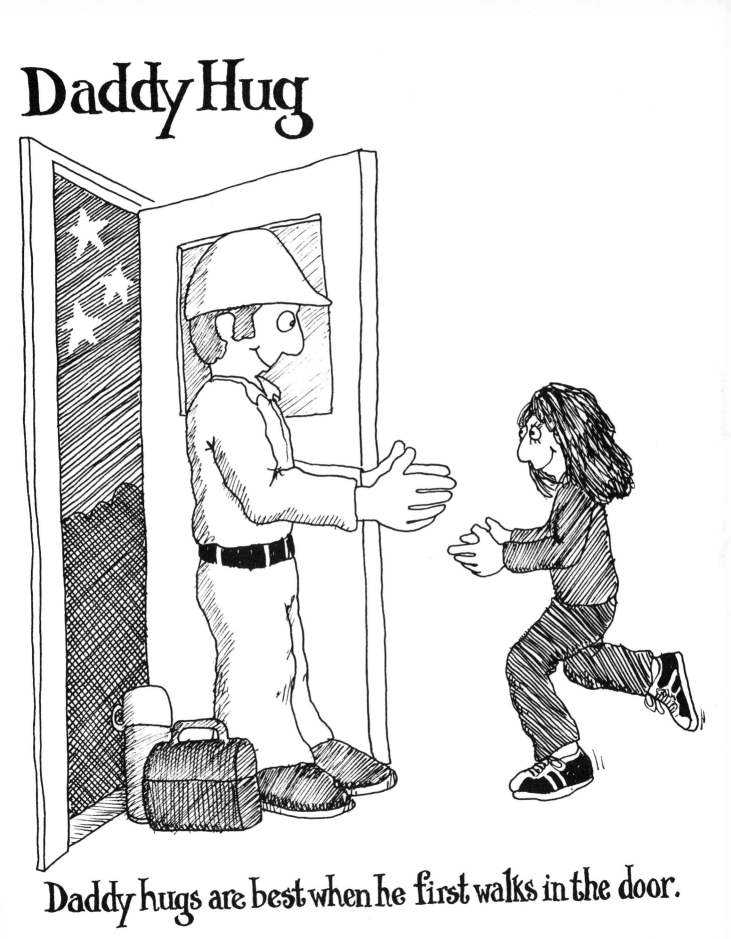

Daddy hugs are best when he first walks in the door.

Grandpa Hugs

Grandpa hugs are sometimes given while sitting.

Grandma Hugs

Grandma hugs can be found anywhere, but are especially nice in the kitchen.

Brother Hug※

※Usually called a Buddy Hug.

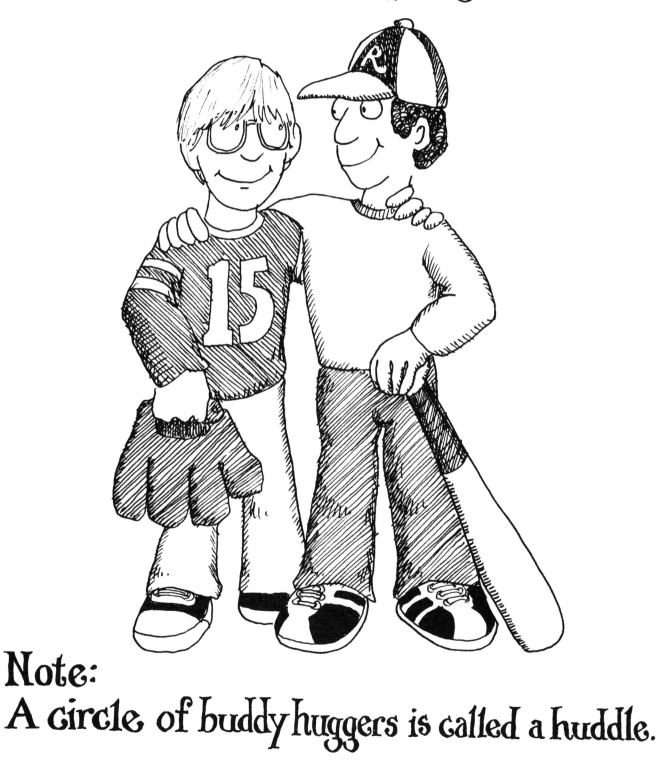

Note:
A circle of buddy huggers is called a huddle.

Sister Hug*
*Also known as a Single-Arm Hug.

Single-arm hugs are good for people who walk together (even if they aren't sisters).

BabyHugs

Baby hugs are given with a little tickle.
(Sometimes they can get you a little wet.)

Great Aunt Mary Hug

A Great Aunt Mary hug can be given by any large lady you see only once a year. (You will usually end up with lipstick on your cheek.)

Arm Hugs

Arm hugs are good for people who are too big for you to get your arms around.

Hand Hugs✳

✳ Usually called holding hands.
  Sometimes called shaking hands.

Never hand-hug with dirty hands unless the other person has dirty hands too.

Knee Hugs

Knee hugs are for tall people.
Warning: Never try to knee-hug a moving person.

Thing Hugs
Blanket Hug

Everyone needs some kind of blanket.

Rock Hugs

BE A LITTLE BOULDER

Rock hugs are very hard on your face.

Pricker Bush Hugs

Never hug a pricker bush. (Or poison ivy or cactus.)

Ice Cube Hug

Ice cube hugs are quite common in February.

Lamppost Hug

A lamppost hug can save you from a painful experience.

Sandwich Hug

The whole family can get into a sandwich hug.

Special Hugs
Birthday Hugs

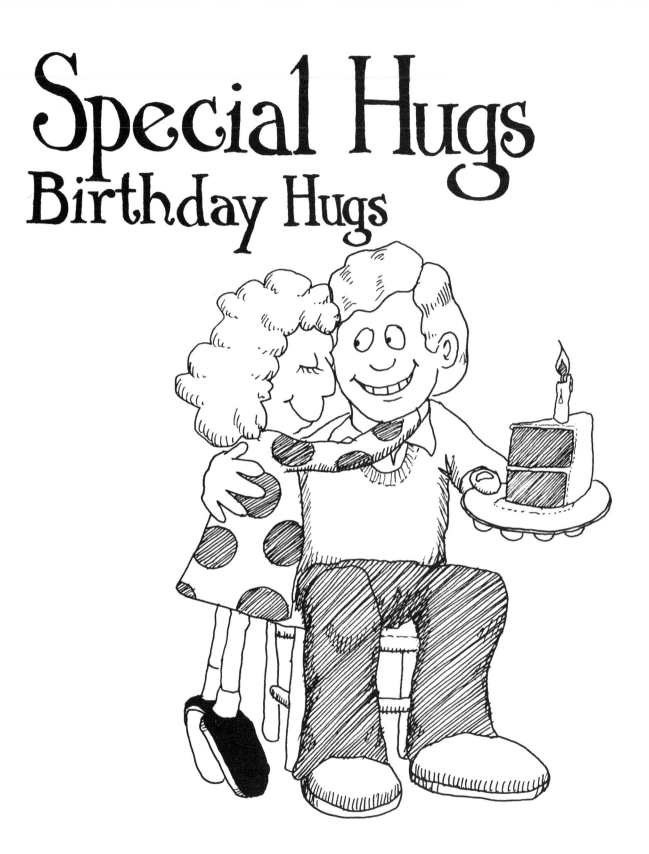

A birthday hug is a present anyone can afford.

Report Card Hugs

A Hug

Bee Hug

Sea Hug

Hurt Hugs

Hurt hugs make the pain go away.

Winner Hugs

Loser Hugs

Facts & Hints About Hugs

There is no such thing as a bad hug:
   there are only good hugs and great hugs.

Hug someone at least once a day and
   twice on a rainy day.

Hug with a smile; closed eyes are optional.

A snuggle is a longish hug.

Bedtime hugs help chase away bad dreams.

Never hug tomorrow someone you could
   hug today.